WHO LOVES THE FALL?

by **Bob Raczka**

illustrated by

Judy Stead

Albert Whitman & Company, Morton Grove, Illinois

For Judy, my favorite librarian, who falls for all of my books.—B.R.

To Nick M. M. and Scott V., my November birthday boys.—J.S.

Also by Bob Raczka and Judy Stead:
Spring Things

Library of Congress Cataloging-in-Publication Data

Raczka, Bob.
Who loves the fall? / by Bob Raczka ; illustrated by Judy Stead.
p. cm.
Summary: Rhyming text and illustrations portray the sights and sounds of autumn,
from "rakers, leapers, and corn-crop reapers" to "trickers, treaters, and turkey eaters."
ISBN 10: 0-8075-9037-1 (hardcover)
ISBN 13: 978-0-8075-9037-9 (hardcover)
[1. Autumn—Fiction. 2. Stories in rhyme.] I. Stead, Judy, ill. II. Title.
PZ8.3.R11153Wh 2007 [E]—dc22 2007001506

The book is set in Stanton.
The design is by Carol Gildar.

For more information about Albert Whitman & Company, please visit our web site at www.albertwhitman.com.

Who loves the fall?

Rakers,

leapers,

corn-crop reapers.

Growers,

pickers,

taffy lickers.

Quilters,

choppers,

helicopters.

Winged migrators,

hibernators.

Hooters,

howlers,

loud meowers.

Bonfire builders,

pie-crust fillers,

even former caterpillars!

Adders,

show-and-tellers.

Passers,

punters,

pumpkin hunters.

Trickers,

treaters,

turkey eaters.

Don't you love the fall?

FALL FACTS

To **reap** means to cut down or harvest a crop, especially tall crops like corn and wheat. In the old days, farmers reaped by hand with curved blades called sickles. Today, they drive big machines with many blades called combines.

A **maple tree** produces seeds that blow free from its branches in the fall. The seeds are shaped like propeller blades. This allows them to spin like helicopters away from the tree, where they have a better chance of growing into new trees.

To **migrate** means to move from one place to another. In the fall, many types of birds migrate from the North to the South, where the winters are warmer. When geese migrate, they fly in large "V" formations and take turns being the leader.

To **hibernate** means to sleep through cold weather. It's how animals like bears survive winter, when food is scarce. In the fall, these animals store up fat in their bodies by eating more. Then they find a den to sleep in and live off the fat until spring.

A **monarch butterfly** starts life as an egg on a milkweed plant. It hatches into a caterpillar, which eats the milkweed leaves. Then it hangs from a twig and transforms into a pupa in a cocoon. Two weeks later, it emerges as a butterfly. In the late summer to early fall, the monarch migrates south.